CITY OF
YORK
COUNCIL

The loan period may be extended by internet, 24-hour telephone renewal line 01904-552833, e-mail, telephone or post, quoting your library I.D., PIN and book barcode.

DRINGHOUSES
6|07
28. JUL
13. OCT
22. FEB
'6. FEB 08
08.

20. SEP 08
25. JUN 09.
07. MAY
21. FEB 11.

D0550001

City of York Libraries	
8888OOOOOO2254	
Askews	02-Apr-2007
JF	£5.99

Author
Gilly Cameron Cooper

Consultant
Nick Saunders

Copyright © ticktock Entertainment Ltd 2007
First published in Great Britain in 2007 by ticktock Media Ltd.,
Unit 2, Orchard Business Centre, North Farm Road,
Tunbridge Wells, Kent, TN2 3XF

ticktock project editor: Jo Hanks
ticktock project designer: Graham Rich

We would like to thank: Indexing Specialists (UK) Ltd.

ISBN 978 1 84696 068 0
Printed in China
A CIP catalogue record for this book is available from the British Library.
All rights reserved. No part of this publication may be reproduced, copied, stored in a retrieval system or
transmitted in any form or by any means electronic, mechanical, photocopying, recording or otherwise without
prior written permission of the copyright owner.

CONTENTS

THE GREEKS, THEIR GODS & MYTHS

The ancient Greeks lived in a world dominated by the Mediterranean Sea, the snow-capped mountains that surrounded it, dangerous winds, and sudden storms. They saw their lives as controlled by the gods and spirits of Nature, and told myths about how the gods fought with each other and created the universe.

It was a world of chance and luck, of magic and superstition, in which the endless myths made sense of a dangerous and unpredictable life.

The ancient Greek gods looked and acted like human beings. They fell in love, were jealous, vain, and argued with each other. Unlike humans, they were immortal. This meant they did not die, but lived forever. They also had superhuman strength and magical powers. Each god had a power that belonged only to them.

In the myths, the gods sometimes had children with humans. These children were born demi-gods and might have special powers, but were usually mortal and could die. When their human children were in trouble, the Olympian gods would help them.

The gods liked to meddle in to human life. Different gods took sides with different people. The gods also liked to play tricks on humans. They did

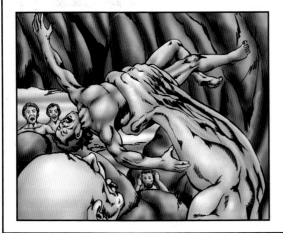

this for all sorts of reasons: because it was fun; because they would gain something; and also for revenge. The Ancient Greeks believed that 12 Olympian gods ruled over the world at any time. The 10 gods and goddesses that you see here were always Olympians, they were the most important ones. Some of them you'll meet in our story.

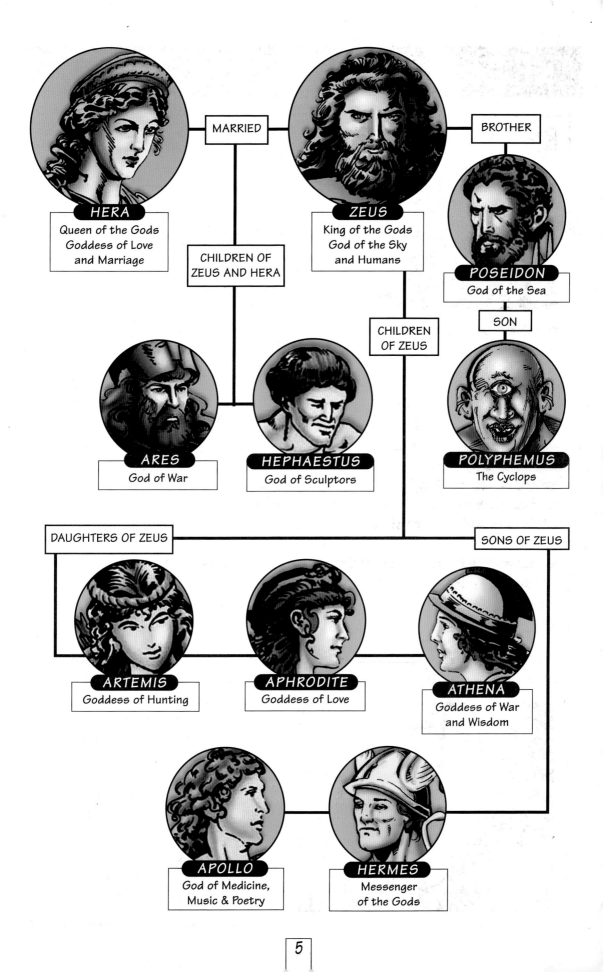

HERA
Queen of the Gods
Goddess of Love
and Marriage

MARRIED

ZEUS
King of the Gods
God of the Sky
and Humans

BROTHER

POSEIDON
God of the Sea

CHILDREN OF
ZEUS AND HERA

CHILDREN
OF ZEUS

SON

ARES
God of War

HEPHAESTUS
God of Sculptors

POLYPHEMUS
The Cyclops

DAUGHTERS OF ZEUS

SONS OF ZEUS

ARTEMIS
Goddess of Hunting

APHRODITE
Goddess of Love

ATHENA
Goddess of War
and Wisdom

APOLLO
God of Medicine,
Music & Poetry

HERMES
Messenger
of the Gods

SETTING THE SCENE

For 10 years Odysseus and his warriors had fought in the Trojan War. The war started because Paris of Troy ran away with the King of Sparta's wife – Helen. The gods had helped the Greeks to win, and the city of Troy was destroyed. But Odysseus and his men had killed many men, unfairly, in the war. So the gods decided that they should be punished. The punishment was to suffer a long and dangerous journey home. The journey put them in many life-threatening situations and introduced them to many strange creatures, including an enchantress, and a one-eyed giant – the Cyclops. Not all of Odysseus' men made it home.

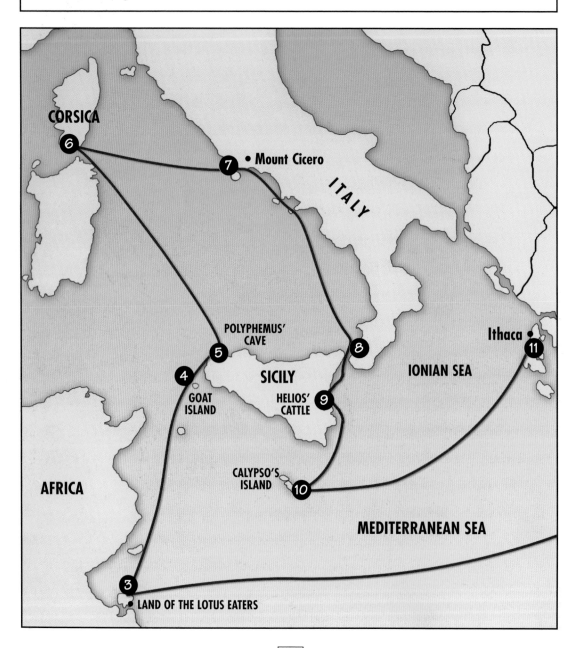

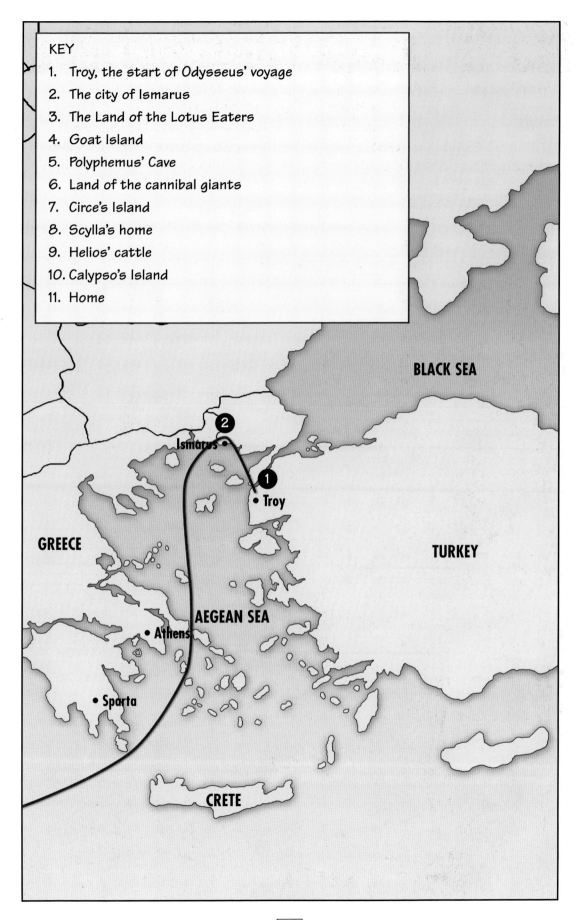

KEY

1. Troy, the start of Odysseus' voyage
2. The city of Ismarus
3. The Land of the Lotus Eaters
4. Goat Island
5. Polyphemus' Cave
6. Land of the cannibal giants
7. Circe's Island
8. Scylla's home
9. Helios' cattle
10. Calypso's Island
11. Home

BLACK SEA

Ismarus

Troy

GREECE

TURKEY

AEGEAN SEA

Athens

Sparta

CRETE

A LONG WAY FROM HOME

After 10 years of fighting in the Trojan Wars, Odysseus and his men wanted to go home to their island of Ithaca. Many years before, a priestess gave Odysseus a message from the gods: 'Fight in the Trojan War, and you will not return home for 20 years.' What dangers and adventures could make their journey last 10 years? Would the gods be on their side, as they had been in the wars?

Ithaca lay southwest of Troy. But Zeus, king of the gods and master of the sky, sent a wind to drive the fleet north.

Forced north, the fleet reached the city of Ismarus. Odysseus and his men thought greedily about the food and treasure they might find there, so decided to sack the city.

It's not time for you to go home yet, Odysseus.

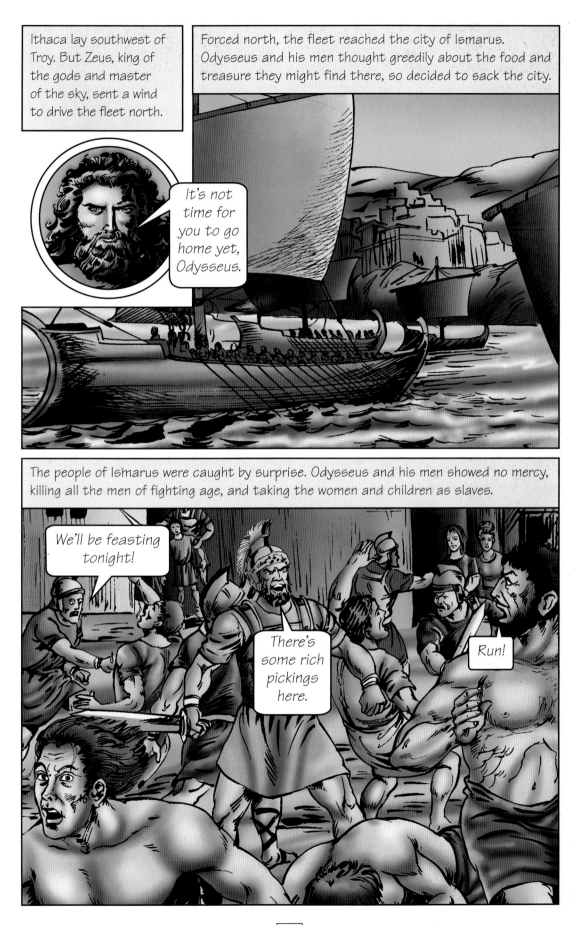

The people of Ismarus were caught by surprise. Odysseus and his men showed no mercy, killing all the men of fighting age, and taking the women and children as slaves.

We'll be feasting tonight!

There's some rich pickings here.

Run!

Near the city, the attackers found Maro, priest to Apollo. Wisely, Odysseus wisely let him, his wife and son live. With the gods already against them, he couldn't risk upsetting Apollo. Maro thanked him with presents, including deliciously strong and sweet red wine, that was to come in very useful later...

Odysseus' men piled up the treasure they had stolen, ready to take on board.

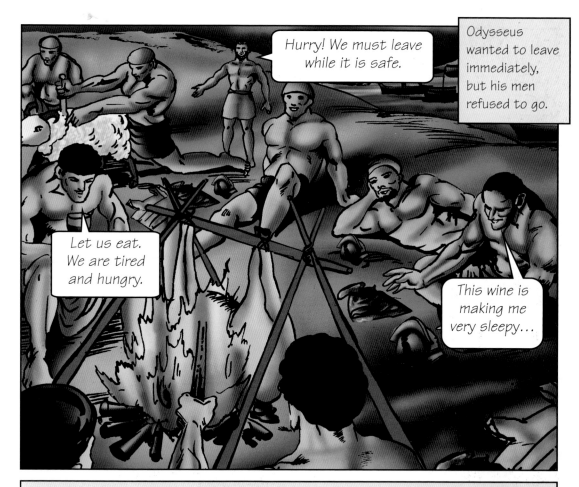

Odysseus wanted to leave immediately, but his men refused to go.

Hurry! We must leave while it is safe.

Let us eat. We are tired and hungry.

This wine is making me very sleepy...

They slept heavily after their feast, to be woken at dawn by a deadly attack. The people from around Ismarus wanted revenge for Odysseus' attack. In the battle six men from each ship were killed before the fleet could escape.

No sooner had they escaped, than the sky darkened with terrifying storm clouds. Zeus was putting another difficulty in their way. For two whole days and nights, gales tore the sails to shreds and waves the size of mountains crashed down on the ships.

No! We will die in these waves!

Will we ever see Ithaca?

I have no strength to fight this storm.

Eventually the storm passed by. But then Zeus sent the ships in the direction of an island. Desperate for fresh water, Odysseus sent three men to find some and report back.

Take great care. We have no idea if the people here are friendly.

The islanders were friendly and offered the three tough warriors bowls of honey-sweet lotus fruit that made them relaxed and happy… and forget about going home.

This fruit is like a drug… I feel so happy.

Mmmm, I just want to be here forever.

Let's stay.

Come on! We must leave straight away, or we'll never get off this island.

Odysseus went in search of his men. When he found them, Odysseus realised the lotus fruit had put them under a spell. He dragged them back to the ships.

A PROMISING LAND

Odysseus and his fleet sailed on, wondering what horrors Zeus and the other gods held in store. One night a heavy fog crept over them, like a grey blanket, until they could not see. The leading ships tossed around on the rolling waters, the lookouts struggling to guide them safely. With hidden rocks all around, they soon ran aground.

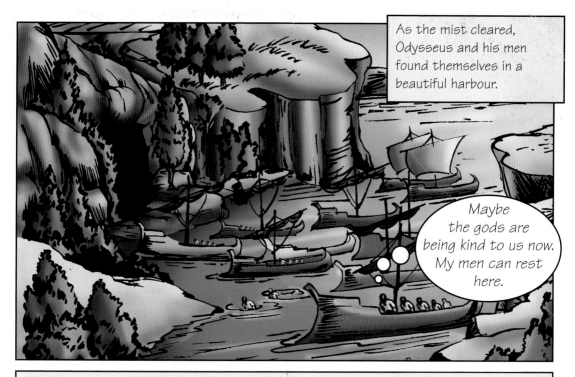

As the mist cleared, Odysseus and his men found themselves in a beautiful harbour.

Maybe the gods are being kind to us now. My men can rest here.

After resting, they set off to hunt for food. The little wooded island had no signs of human life. There were only goats, hundreds of them, that didn't know to be frightened of humans...

Look, there's another... and another... they're everywhere! We'll eat well tonight.

As they tucked into their roasted goats, the men gazed over the water to a bigger island. It was obvious that someone lived there from the rising smoke and bleating sheep.

I'll take one ship over to see what the people are like. The rest of you stay here.

Odysseus and his crew saw a jagged cliff with a gaping cave at its base. In front were animal pens. They moored the ship in a hidden cove.

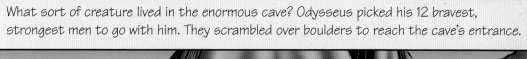

What sort of creature lived in the enormous cave? Odysseus picked his 12 bravest, strongest men to go with him. They scrambled over boulders to reach the cave's entrance.

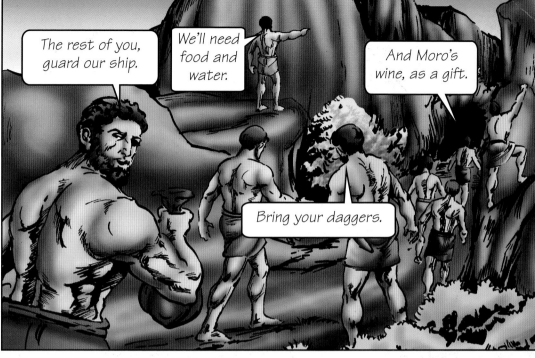

There was no-one at home. The rocks making the animal pen were enormous. It must have taken someone very large and strong to lift them.

THE CYCLOPS COMES HOME

The men crept into the cave to find baskets of cheese, buckets of milk and more animals in pens. The men wanted to steal some food then return to the ship, but Odysseus insisted they stay to find out who lived there. After all, Odysseus thought, the gods' ruled that guests, invited or not, must be treated well. So they waited, cooking some lambs to eat.

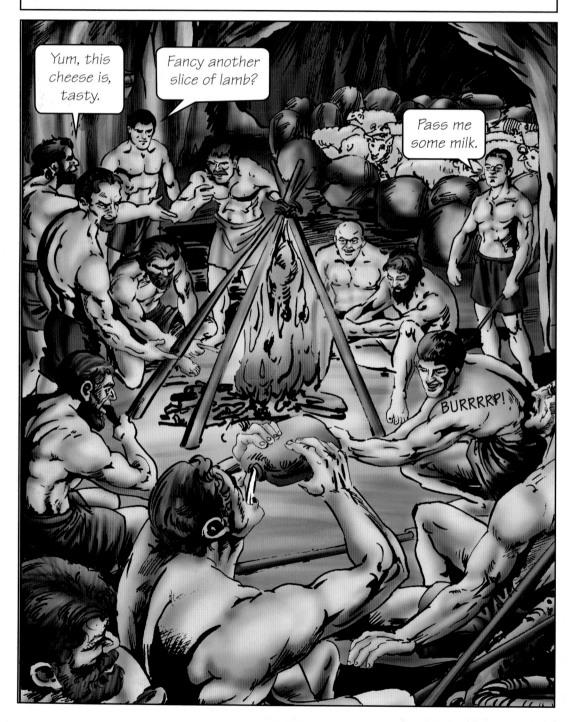

Suddenly, heavy footsteps shook the cave. The hideous bulk of a giant filled the entrance. It was Polyphemus, a Cyclops, who was known to enjoy the taste of humans. A single bulbous eye moved in the centre of his forehead. He didn't notice the men.

I'm so tired of eating nothing but goats and sheep.

Oh, no... it's a Cyclops, they hate humans.

Polyphemus lit a fire before picking up an enormous slab of stone that he used as a door. It was so big that 20 oxen couldn't have moved it. He placed it over the cave entrance. As he turned, he caught sight of his visitors in the flickering firelight.

Odysseus' heart sank into his sandals as he faced the Cyclops. He bravely explained that they had been driven off course as they returned home from Troy.

Don't forget, the gods punish those who do not welcome travellers.

Polyphemus sneered. Then he grabbed two men, one after the other. With his sharp teeth he tore them limb from limb, and ate them raw – bones and all...

Aaaarrrgh!

Huh, what makes you think I care about gods or guests? We Cyclopes are stronger than any god.

Polyphemus lay down on his bed, closed his eye and was soon snoring loudly. Odysseus and his men could do nothing but pray to Zeus, although he hadn't helped them so far. Even if they killed the Cyclops, they would never be able to move the great rock blocking the cave entrance.

Show us mercy, oh great gods! Help us find a way out of here.

Zzzzzzzzzzz

Finally, beams of morning light squeezed through the cracks around the giant slab.

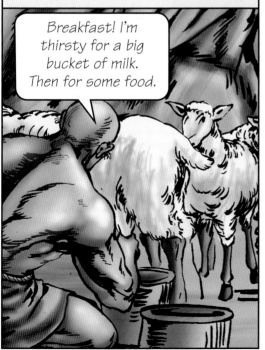

Breakfast! I'm thirsty for a big bucket of milk. Then for some food.

Polyphemus' huge hand reached out and grabbed another two men.

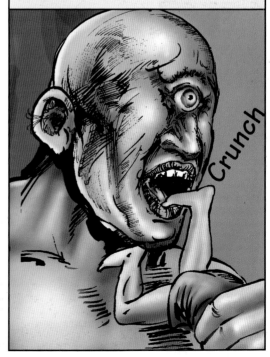

Crunch

Then, Polyphemus lifted the great stone from the entrance as if it was a pebble. He stepped into the morning sun, with his flock before him. For a moment Odysseus and his men saw the glittering turquoise sea and freedom...

... but the Cyclops turned to slip the boulder back in place, and once again they were trapped in darkness.

He'll eat us one by one...

I must come up with a plan to get us out of here... before we are all eaten alive!

Odysseus set his men to work. Some lit a fire. Others found a tree trunk and used their daggers to shave one end to a point.

Together they hardened the tip in the fire, until it was as strong as steel. Then they hid the giant stake beneath the piles of dung heaped around the cave.

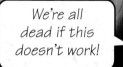

We're all dead if this doesn't work!

In the darkness, they waited quietly for Polyphemus' return. Would Odysseus' plan work?

OUTWITTING THE CYCLOPS

Evening fell and finally Polyphemus returned. He herded his animals into the cave, and put back the entrance stone. Odysseus felt sick when the Cyclops grabbed and ate another two of his warriors. It was time to start the plan. Remember the wine that Maro, the priest of Ismarus, had given the travellers? Odysseus filled a bowl with it and handed it to the Cyclops.

Polyphemus greedily gulped the wine and demanded more. Three bowls later, he was drunk and started talking. When asked his name, clever Odysseus told the Cyclops his name was 'Odeia'... which meant 'nobody'.

My nickname is Odeia.

I like this. Gi' me more. Hic! Tell me, what's yer name? **Buuurrrrp!**

Well, Odeia, I have a special treat for you... ha, ha, ha.

My present to you is that I'll eat yer last... very slowly... **ha, ha, ha.**

With that, the drunken Cyclops fell over, unconscious. Odysseus' plan was working.

Splat

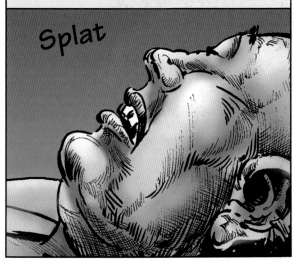

Hurriedly the men grabbed the stake, and laid the point in the Cyclops' fire until it glowed red-hot.

Odysseus and his remaining men picked it up. Holding it firm, they charged at the sleeping Cyclops and rammed the sizzling point into his eye.

All together... *push!*

Sizzle

Crackle

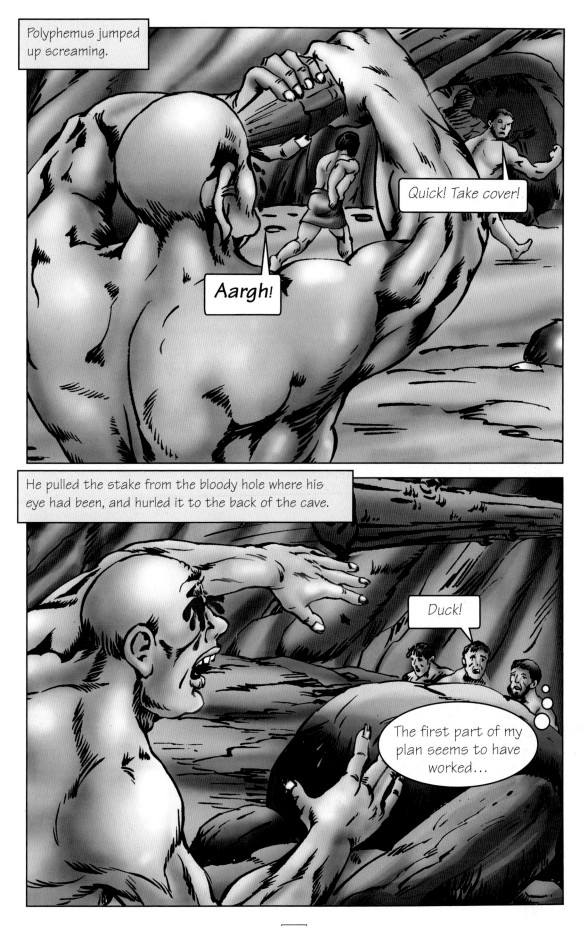

Polyphemus jumped up screaming.

Quick! Take cover!

Aargh!

He pulled the stake from the bloody hole where his eye had been, and hurled it to the back of the cave.

Duck!

The first part of my plan seems to have worked...

27

BLIND MAN'S BLUFF

In the moonlight, Polyphemus set himself in front of the cave entrance groaning quietly in pain. He blocked the light, and Odysseus' hopes of escape. The Cyclops' enormous hands swept the ground around him, feeling to make sure no human could slip past.

Odysseus racked his brains for some way to get around the Cyclops. He thought of the branches that made up Polyphemus' bed… and the big, fleecy rams.

Maybe that will work… men, pray for help! I have an idea…

Of course, Odysseus came up with an idea – he always did. Odysseus caught three of the biggest rams. He tied them together with branches from the giant's bed.

I must work quickly and quietly, before Polyphemus realises anything.

Odysseus tied together five more ram teams. Finally there was one team for each of his surviving men. Each warrior slid under the middle ram in his team, and Odysseus strapped his men in.

For himself, Odysseus took the biggest ram of all. He squeezed beneath its belly, and held on to the thick fleece for dear life.

As the sun rose, the rams walked to the mouth of the cave, ready to go to the fields. As they passed Polyphemus, the Cyclops ran his hands over their backs. He wanted to make sure no-one was riding them, but he didn't check underneath. Soon all the rams were out in the open, leaving only the biggest one carrying Odysseus. The brave warrior held his breath as Polyphemus spoke to the ram.

You are the strongest of my flock, why are you so slow today? Do you stay to protect your blinded master? I'll get that Mr Odeia yet and eat him slowly.

PARTING SHOT

Odysseus and his men were on their way to safety. The men rowed fast and a breeze soon caught the sails. The ship sliced quickly through the waves. Odysseus saw Polyphemus stumble onto the cliffs behind them.

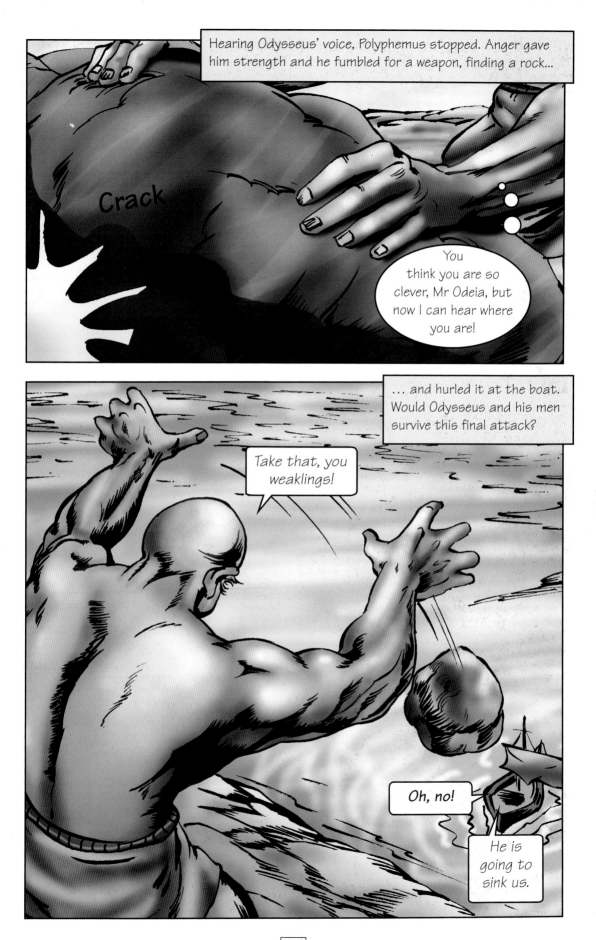

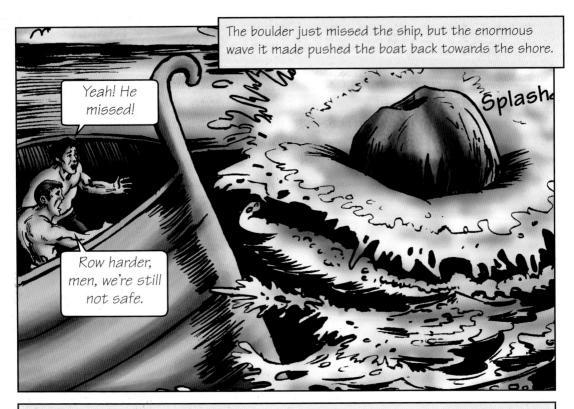

Back on the first island, Odysseus and his entire fleet ate the Cyclops' sheep and drank wine. They thanked the gods for their safety. Odysseus sacrificed the big black ram, offering it to Zeus in return for safe passage to Ithaca.

POSEIDON'S REVENGE

It was soon obvious that Odysseus' sacrifice and prayers were not enough. Zeus could see no reason to change his mind. The travellers' journey would carry on to be long, hard and dangerous. Now that Odysseus had also angered Poseidon, by blinding his son, more danger would come their way.

First, on the island of Corsica, cannibalistic giants killed many of Odysseus' men. Only Odysseus and his ship's crew escaped. The survivors took to the seas in a single ship.

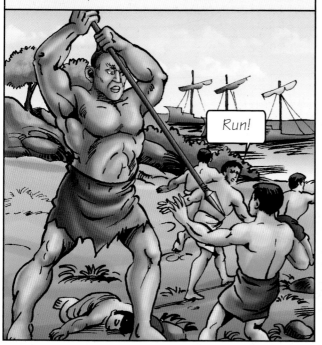

Next Circe, a beautiful enchantress, lured them to her island and turned them into boars. Odysseus' charm finally persuaded her to make them men again.

After getting away from Circe, the men dodged a deadly whirlpool. In doing so they sailed in reach of the six-headed monster, Scylla. A man was lost to each head. Worse, though, was yet to come…

On Helios' island, eating cattle was forbidden. Trapped there by bad weather, Odysseus' men ran out of food so ate some cows. Enraged, Helios complained to Zeus who raised a terrible storm when they were back at sea, destroying the last ship and killing the rest of Odysseus' crew.

As you did not eat the meat Odysseus, I cannot punish you.

So Odysseus was left on his own. Clinging to a piece of wood, he drifted to the enchantress Calypso's land. Calypso kept Odysseus as a prisoner for seven years, despite his pleas to go home to Ithaca. Eventually, the other gods felt sorry for Odysseus and persuaded Calypso to let Odysseus go.

Odysseus arrived home to find his son, Telemachus, had grown up and his lovely wife Penelope still waiting for him. 20 years after he set off, having battled countless monsters, the gods finally agreed that Odysseus had paid his price for fighting in the Trojan War. He lived many happy years on Ithaca.

Cannibalistic: *man-eating.*

Charybdis: *a whirlpool in the narrow Strait of Messina that sucked ships to the ocean floor. If you escaped Charybdis, you would be in danger of being caught by Scylla, a six-headed monster.*

Circe: *an ancient Greek enchantress who could turn men into animals.*

Cove: *a small bay on the coastline.*

Cyclopes: *nasty, one-eyed giants.*

Dung: *manure.*

Enchantress: *a woman who can make magic. She can use spells to control other people.*

Fleece: *a sheep's wool coat.*

Fleet: *a group of ships.*

Herd: *a group of animals.*

Immortal: *living forever, with no death, like the gods.*

Kindle: *to set something on fire.*

Lotus fruit: *a mythical fruit that makes people relax and forget things.*

Mercy: *to forgive someone for something they have done wrong.*

Moor: *to park a ship.*

Mortal: *having a life that is ended by death, usually referring to humans as being different from immortal gods.*

Myths: *the stories of a tribe or people that tell of their gods, heroes and turning points in their history.*

Olympian: *describes the 12 Greek gods who lived on Mount Olympus in northern Greece, headed by Zeus, and including Poseidon and Athena.*

Passage: *a sea journey.*

Pen: *a place where animals are kept together, usually surrounded by a fence or wall.*

Priest/priestess: *a man or woman who devotes his or her life to serving a god or gods.*

Puny: *small and weak.*

Ram: *a male sheep.*

Revenge: *getting your own back on someone who has harmed you, or for someone you care about.*

Sack: *to attack, destroy and plunder a city or building.*

Sacrifice: *an offering, such as a specially killed animal, to a god in the hope of winning the god's support.*

Scylla: *a six-headed female monster who lived in the Straits of Messina between the southern tip of Italy and Sicily. If sailors escaped the whirlpool of Charybdis on the other side of the channel, they fell into the deadly clutches of Scylla.*

Spare: *to let someone go, without hurting them.*

Trojan War: *the war of all the Greek kingdoms against the city-state of Troy. It began when Helen, the most beautiful woman in the ancient world, left her Spartan husband, Menelaus for Paris, prince of Troy. Odysseus and his men were one of the Greek forces to fight at Troy. The war lasted 10 years before the Greeks finally won.*

Troy: *the city-state where the Trojan Wars were fought.*

Unconscious: *to be asleep, or knocked out.*

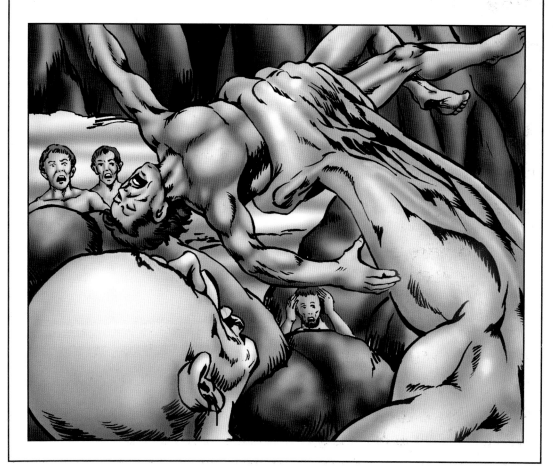

INDEX